ISBN: 978-1-7364829-2-6 (Paperback)

Published by

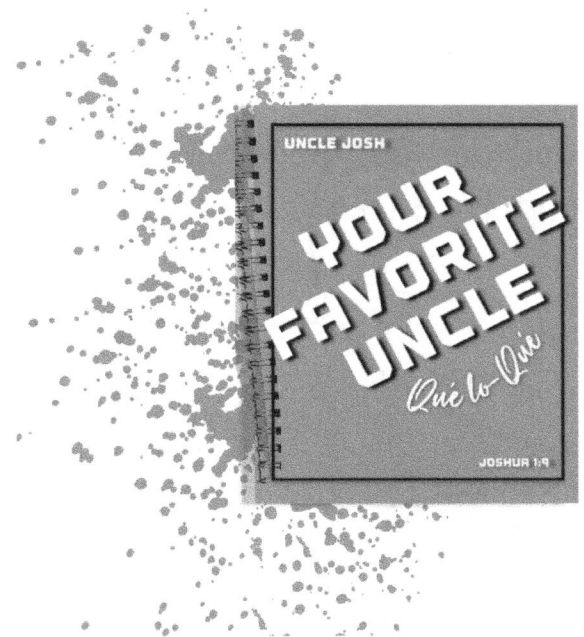

Publisher Consultant

SOPHISTICATED
PRESS

FAMINE

MOABOLIS
YES   NO

Elime looking down with a shocking revelation.

Naomi picks his face up with her hands and holds it.

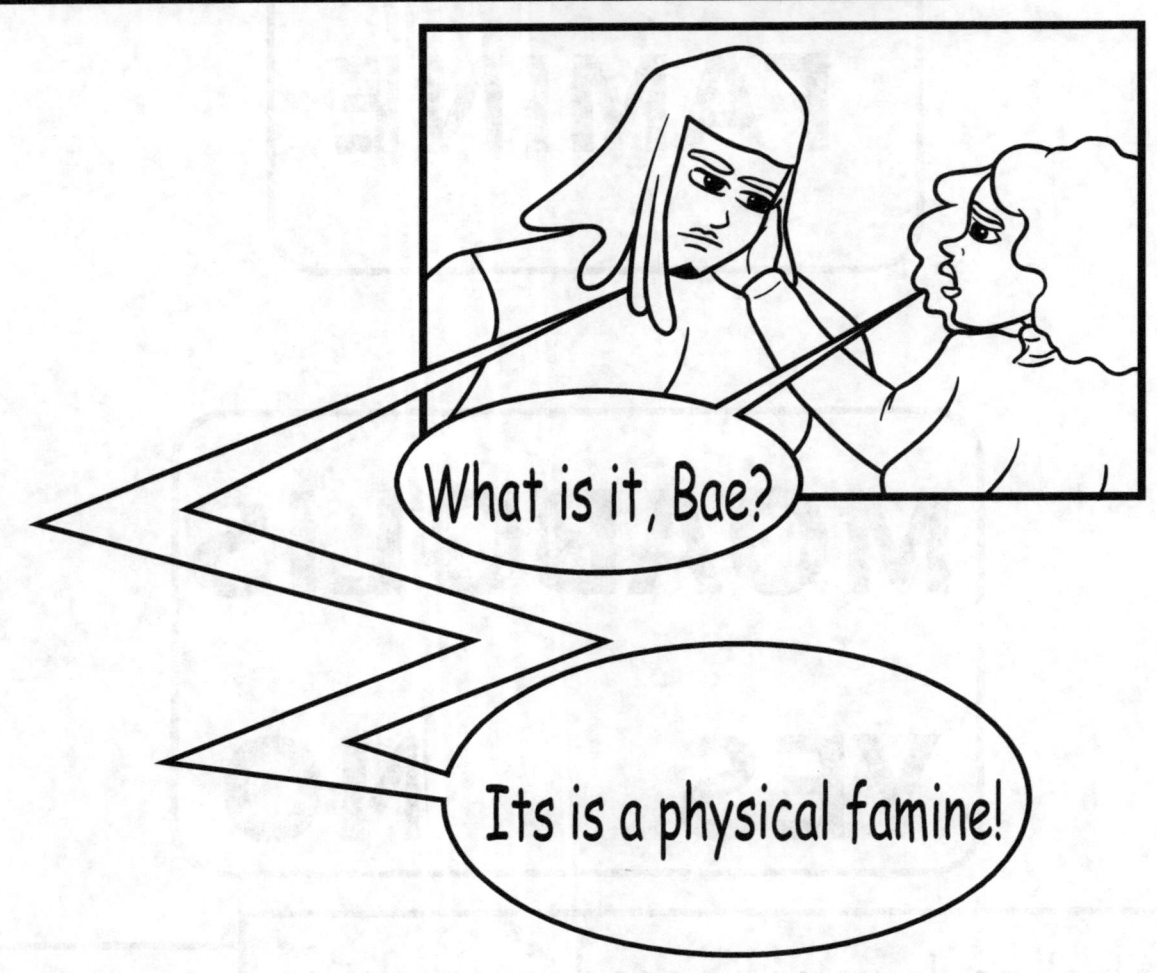

What is it, Bae?

Its is a physical famine!

Look of shock and panic shows on the faces of Mahlon, Naomi, & Emile!

Elime removes Naomi's hand and proceeds towards the screen.

Elime's finger is screen drawing back as the "Yes" button has been pushed.

The screen disappears. Elime looks relieved but his family does not.

So, what now?

Now, we start packin'.

Elime starts to walk down the hallway confidently but is stopped by an invisible bubble.

Elime stumbles back a little.

Elime, slightly frustrated,
charges at the invisible bubble
with force.

And falls back on his butt.

Naomi crouches down as he is rubbing his head.

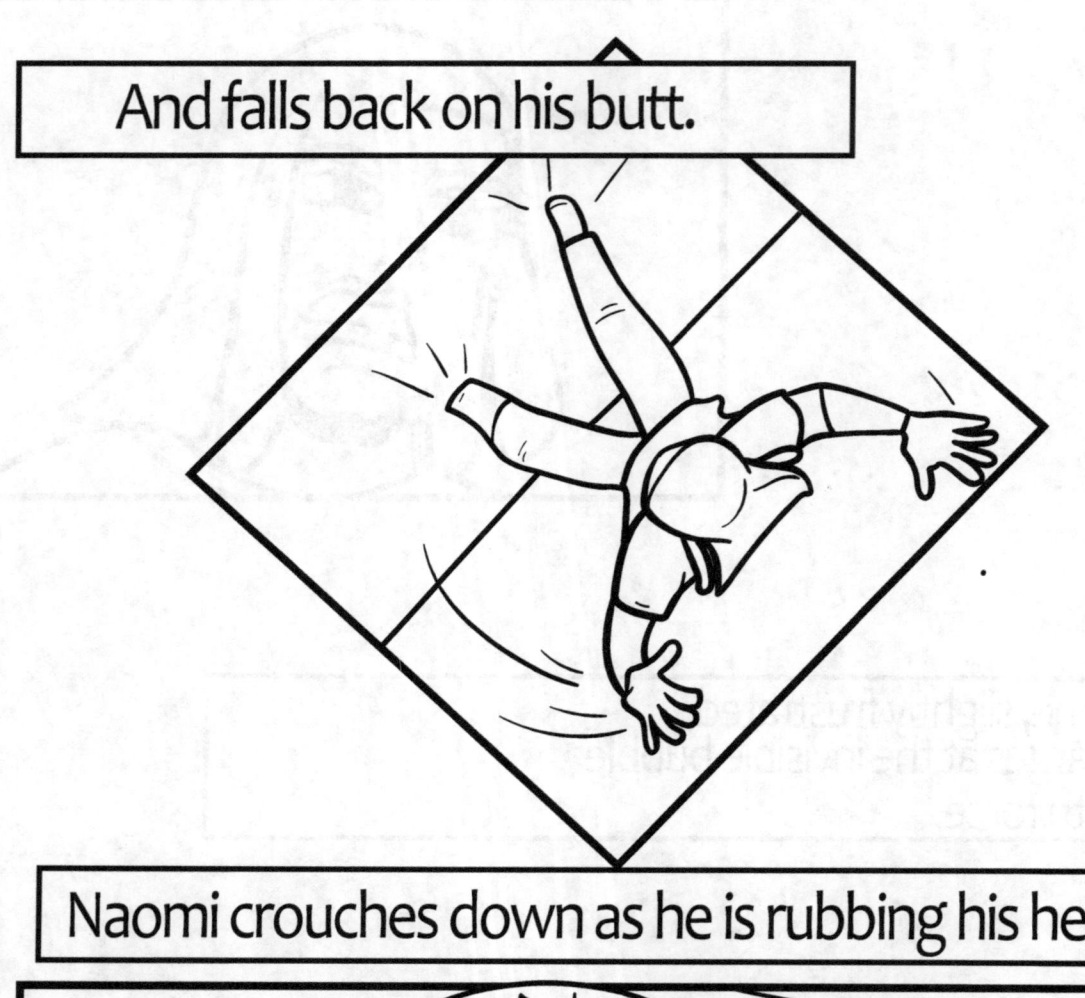

The family is kicking and hitting trying to break the force field.

BANG!
BANG!
BANG!

Suddenly, the entire house goes dark
only the area in the force field has light. The family is confused.

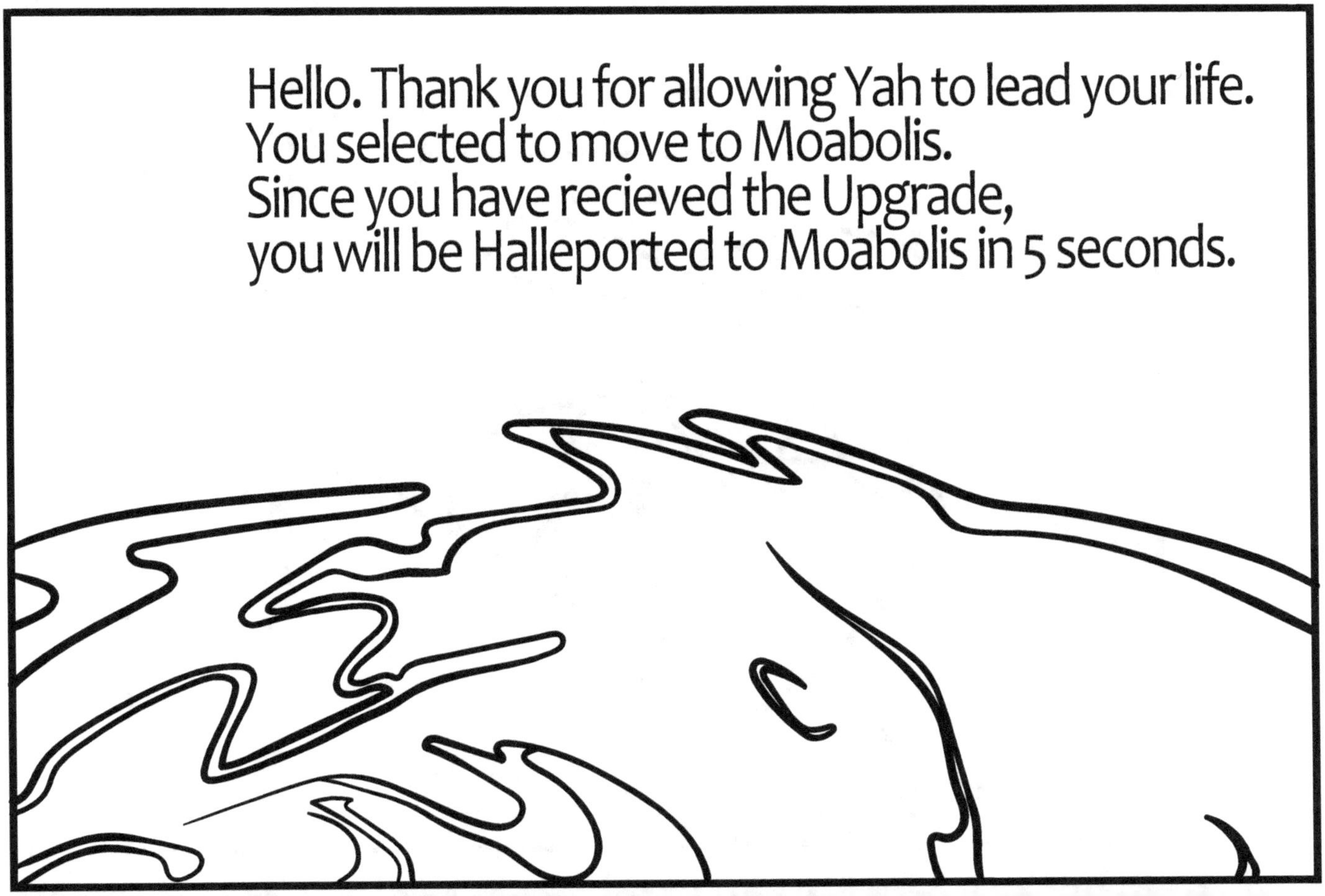

Hello. Thank you for allowing Yah to lead your life.
You selected to move to Moabolis.
Since you have recieved the Upgrade,
you will be Halleported to Moabolis in 5 seconds.

Family looking around trying to determine where that voice is coming from.
Everything is dark but their Hallelujahs have light.

" I mean at the end of this broadcast,
you all will be uploaded into our servers and downloaded straight to Moabolis.
Once again, thank you for allowing Yah to lead your life and remember, Keep Believing".

Sheer panic is shown across the faces of Elime and his family
as they continuously kick and punch the bubble.

The entire room is pitch black,
except a "5" second countdown clock suddenly appears on the bubble.
The kicking and punching stop completely.

The kicking and punching start back up.

"Actually, there is. We can belieeeeve."

1

Elime is seen grabbing hold his family and they all bunch together, uncertain for what is next. A giant black hole has opened and is sucking the family up.

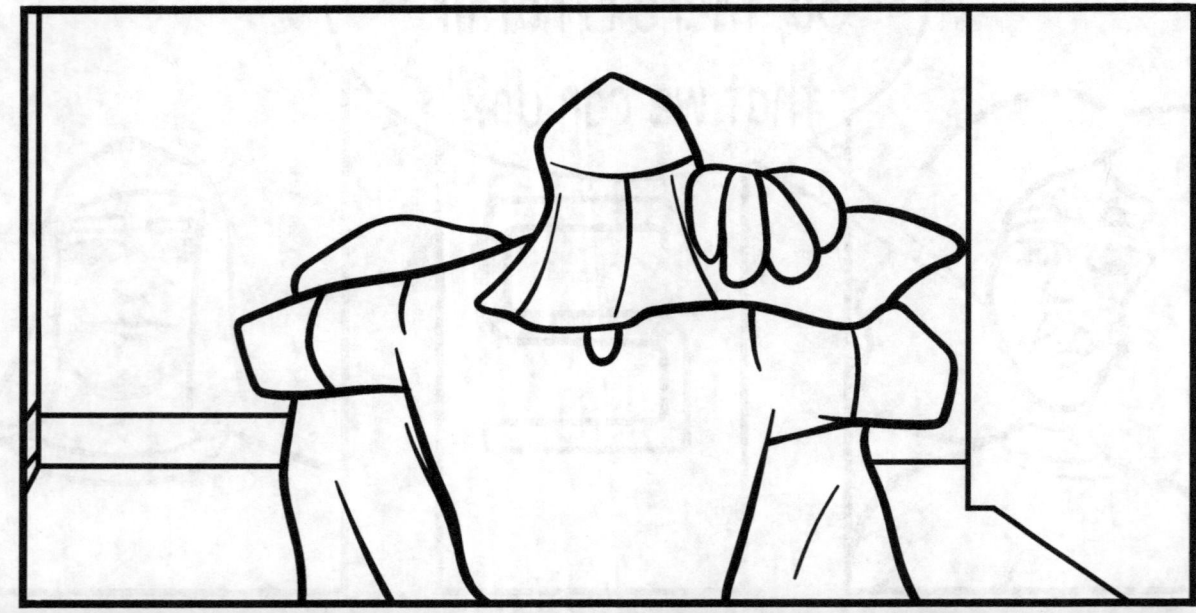

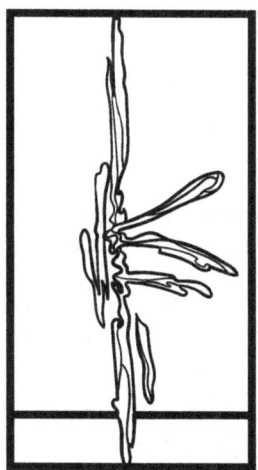 # SLLLRRRP

The family is now flying though a tunnel of pix- elated feathers that glow.
They still remained holding on to each other and
they kept their eyes closed tightly. Their screams are muffled.

A black hole tears open the sky in a dimly lit aley with graffiti on the building.
The family is thrown out and lands safely on their feet.
They are still holding tightly to each other and their screams are fading.

Building withe graffiti. Trash cans and dumpters.
The family lands inside of an alley. A modern, metropolitan, futuristic city.
Elime lifts his head nervously and lets his family go. He looks relieved that evrything is okay.
The ithers let go and look relieved but confused as they examine their sorroundings.

MOABOLIS!

Dad, what do we do now?

Everyone is focused on Elime and they are confused and lost at what to do now.

The only thing we can do, son. Ask Yah for help

Hallelujah spat a message out as soon as he uttered those words!

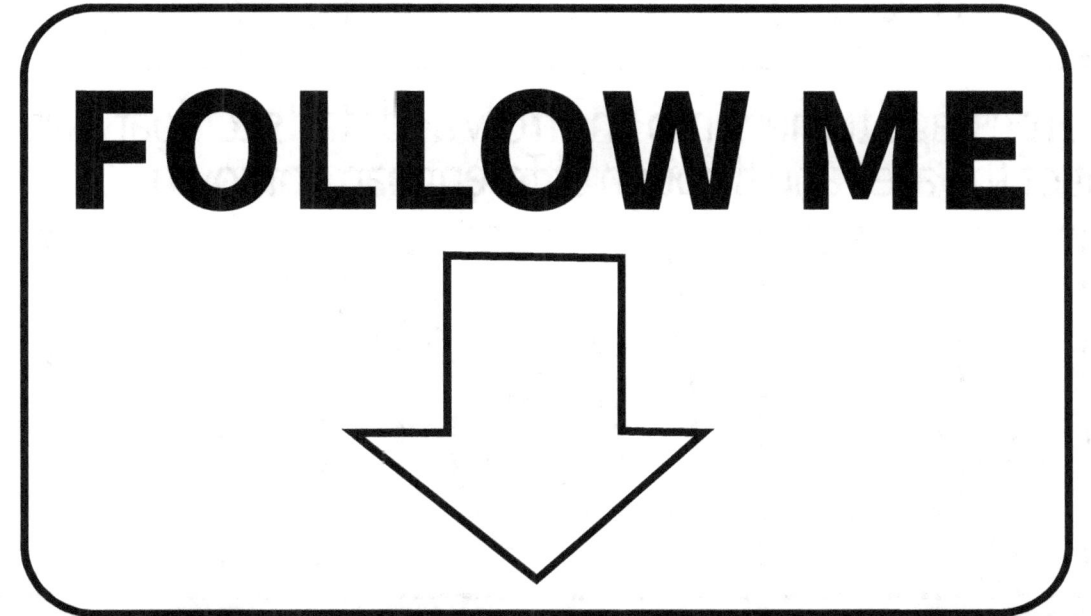

FOLLOW ME

Family looks at one another confused and unsure at what to do next, with the exception of Elime.

The message turners into an arrow and starts to float away out of the alley and through different parts of town.

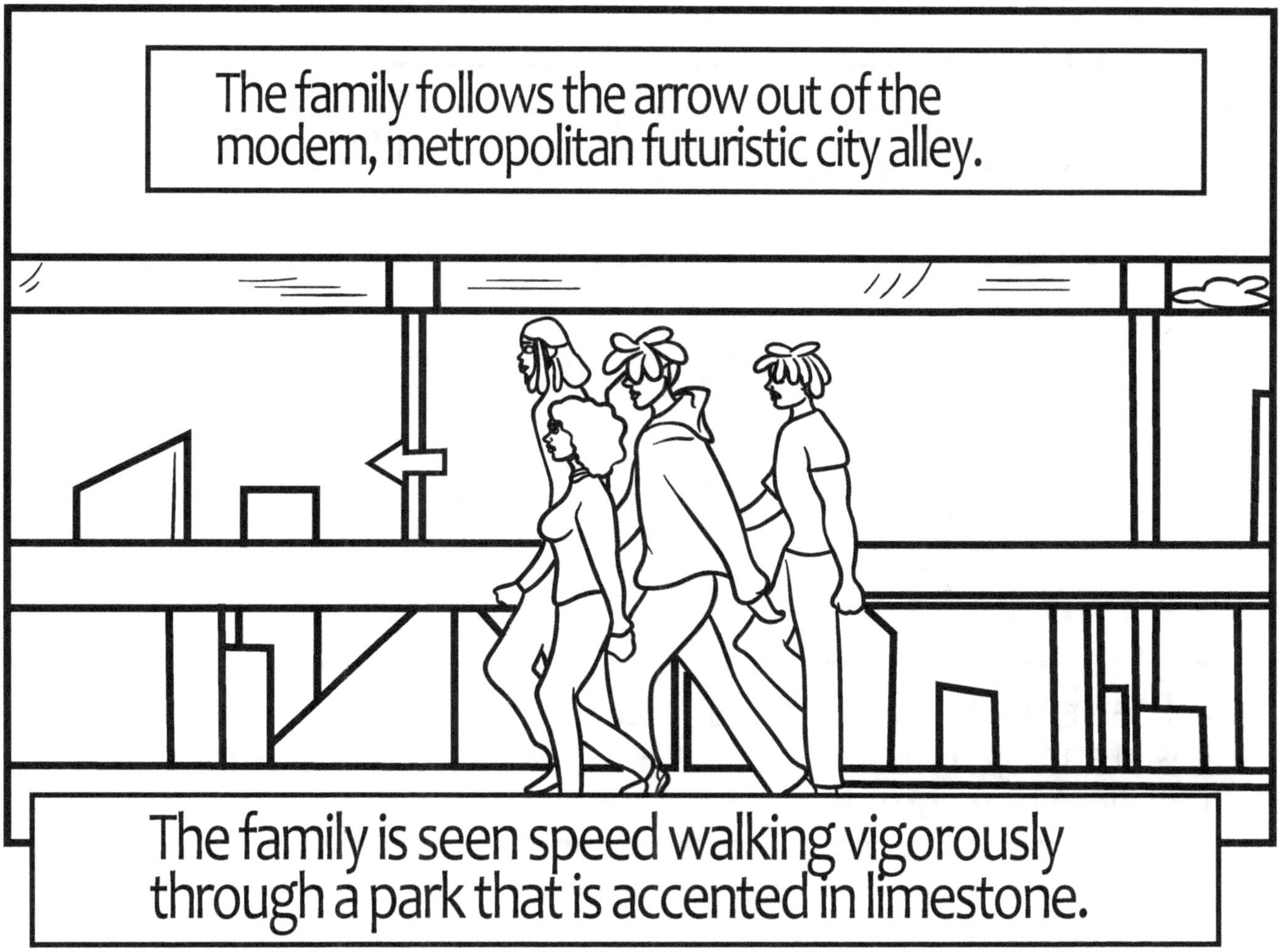

The family follows the arrow out of the modern, metropolitan futuristic city alley.

The family is seen speed walking vigorously through a park that is accented in limestone.

The family is seen climbing over a two- story building during work hours and there are people watching in the city and building watching. Everyone has a shocked look on their face but the family

The arrow has brought them to a door of what looks to be an abandonded warehouse on the other side of time in the more futuristic/technologically heavy art of the city. The area is vacant. Tha arrow makes a sign on the door.

The arrow has vanished and Eilime is standing in front of the door and the family is standing behind him completely nervous.

This must be home!

How do you know this is home?

PSALM 119:105

He walks closer to the door and it opens automatically. Elime smiles.

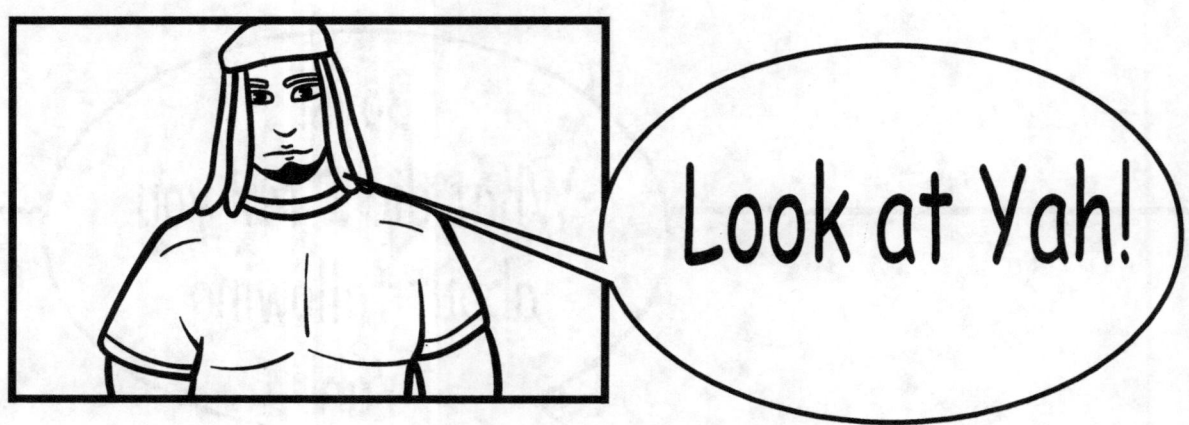

Elime motions his family to come into the brightly lit warehouse with him and they follow him right along, trusting him.

Welcome to the home of The Efrathats

The family was shocked in disbelief as they saw a state-of-the-art super technologically advanced home. The furniture is green and everything is voice activated, capable of human speech, and can float.

The family was still in shock as a floating tray with drinks approached them. They took it one-by-one before the tray floated away.

Elime was finished taking sip of his fruit juice.

The family is walking on the tiled floor that heats up with every step, towards the couch that is now red.

The family places their drinks on their floating trays

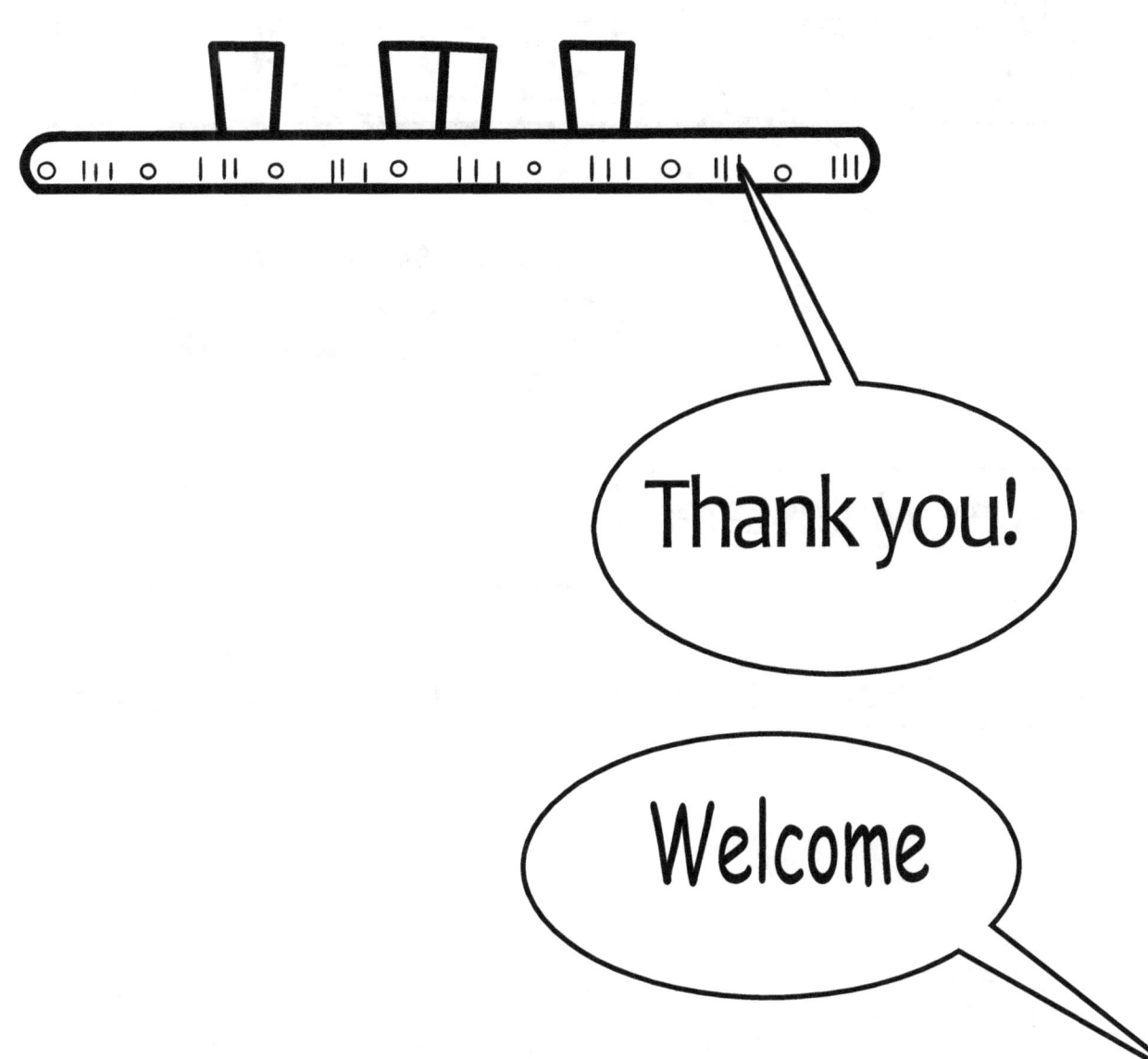

The family recline in their seat,
sleep and have a pleasant look on their faces
as the crazy day is finally over.

Chapter 2

Three Moths Later

Elime lounging on the blue sofa.
Elime shakes his Hallelujah slightly on his right arm and a Hologram spats out.
Elime sits up properly and begins checking the analytics's of his business.

Naomi struts into
the room in K.E.3's stilettos
(balsam flower on the shoe)
with matching, more form fitting,
royal blue and white tracksuit.

They smile at each other and she curls next to him.
They both feel warm and fuzzy on the inside.

A sudden of expression is on Elime's face as he recieves an email that he had not expected.
ELIME: (BREATHES IN HEAVENLY)

Elime and his wife in suspiciously to read the subject to make sure it is real.

' King Eglon Summons You'

About The Author

Joshua Fordham thrives as a digital storyteller, editor, and educational coach. He possesses a B.A. in Spanish, an M.S. in Education, and has been an educational coach in the subject of English for the last five years. In the realm of digital storytelling, he focuses on Afro-Futurism and the effect it can have on inspiring millennials to learn more about the Bible. In the realm of editing, his goal is to edit other documents and show others tips on how to autocorrect in real-time. Finally, in the realm of educational coach, he believes that people learn best by doing as it is innately in them.

For collaboration opportunities please visit
www.yourfavoriteuncle.com